The Tale of the Round Box on the Square Table

By Casey Robert Swanson

isbn 979-8-9948102-0-0

SageAuthorBooks.
www.sageauthorbooks.com

This story was written for my niece and nephew, Lisa and
Elliott, when they were tiny tots, way back in the late 1970's.
I was studying in the cafeteria under the library
at the Univeristy of Washington. As I was studying I noticed on
a table near-bye a blue round box with a green lid sitting on it.
That inspired this story.
So I guess you can say this story is true.

This book is dedicated to Lisa, Elliott, my grandson Eiro, my
granddaughter, MaryAlice and all of the kids of the world.

The round box sat on the square table. No one knew why it was there. The round box just looked like it belonged on the square table.

The round box sat on the square table for a long time.
People walked by the table all of the time. They even sat
down at the table, but the poor box remained undistrubed.

Nobody knew who put the round box on the square table. Not that it mattered anymore. Because the person who put the round box on the square table had forgotten about the box a long time ago.

Days passed and nightimes too. And the round box sat sad, but contently on the square table, waiting, just waiting, for somebody to pick it up. But no one did.

The round box began to worry, as boxes have been known to do. Why had nobody picked it up, or at least lifted its oversize lid to see what was inside. But people just walked on by , or even sat at the table, ignoring the round box on the square table.

The box wanted to cry out, "Please, will somebody pick me up and look inside of me." But nobody heard because as everybody knows, people can't hear what a box is saying

The square table was used all of the time. People sat around the table talking, with their books piled up high around the box. But nobody picked up the box and nobody looked inside to see what lay in the box.

The box thought to itself, 'Am I not a pretty box, as blue as the sky through the windows.'

And the box continued to think to itself, 'Don't I have a magnificent green lid, though slightly oversized, as green as the tree through the window.'

'Am I not large,' thought the box, 'big enough to carry anything that people might want to put inside me.'

But people still ignored the round box on the square table and the box felt lonely. And the box would have cried if a box could cry.

More days passed, and then weeks, and still the round box sat on the square table. People continued to gather around the table upon which the box sat. Still they refused to pick up the box or look inside of the lonely, lonely box.

The sky outside the window that the box looked out had now changed to grey and the box could see snow on the ground through the window.

The box felt cold and damp, like it had never felt before. And the box was sad. 'Will nobody ever pick me up, such a pretty box am I?' Still nobody picked up the box and fewer people gathered around the square table every day.

It remained this way for several more days. Until, one day, a little boy walking with his mother and father, saw the pretty round box sitting on the square table. And he picked it up.

"Mommy, Daddy," the little boy yelled in delight. "A box for my present to my sister. It's perfect. The little boy held the box close to himself and hugged it. And the pretty round box was happy.

"Is there anything in the box?" the father asked the little boy."

The little boy carefully put the round box back on the square table, lifted its oversize lid and, as nobody had done before, looked inside the round box.

"It's empty!" the little boy happily called out, once again picking up the round box after first carefully setting its oversize lid back into place.

For the box was indeed empty, as everybody who had seen it sitting on the square table had known. That is why nobody had picked up the round box and looked inside. After all, who would leave a round box sitting on a square table if there was anything inside the box.

The little boy carried the box home. There he filled it with his love and a present for his sister. The round box, which had sat so long on the square table, was no longer empty. And the pretty blue round box with the slightly oversized green lid was very happy.

Finally the boy put the blue round box with the green lid under a tree. A tree like the box had seen through the window when it sat on the square table for so long. There the box joined other pretty boxes.

And it a box could smile, and maybe they can, the round blue box with the slightly oversized green lid, that sat so long alone on the square table, would have the biggest smile that a box could have.